The Three Musketeers

Written by Alexandre Dumas

Retold by Martin Howard

Illustrated by Ludovic

Collins

D1610500

1 No one laughs at me

On a bright spring day, in the year 1625, a young
traveller rode into a small village in France.
Behind him, people spilled from their houses,
pointing and jeering. The villagers had never seen
such a peculiar sight. The young man was ordinary –
though handsome and bold – with a droopy feather in
his cap and a battered sword at his hip. But he rode
a bandy-legged and ugly old horse, which had
no tail and a strange yellow coat.

1625

The young man – whose name was d'Artagnan –
scowled. He was travelling to Paris in the hope of joining
the King's Musketeers, the finest and proudest soldiers
in all of France. Musketeers never ignored insults
– no one was going to laugh at him and his horse!
Jumping to the ground outside an inn, he spotted yet
another man laughing through the window.

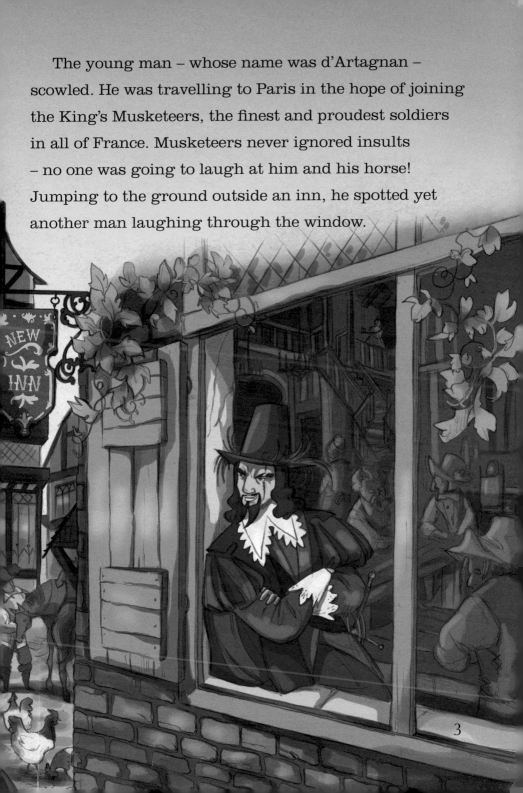

D'Artagnan rested his hand on the hilt of his sword. "You, sir!" he shouted. "Why are you laughing?"

The dark-haired stranger was dressed in fine clothes and had a scar on his cheek. "Mind your own business," he sneered.

"I find your laughter insulting," growled d'Artagnan.

The dark stranger stepped out of the inn. "I laugh at whatever I like," he replied.

D'Artagnan's sword flashed in his hand. "*No one* laughs at me," he cried. "Defend yourself!"

The dark man jumped away as d'Artagnan lunged. "You're mad, boy," he said, snapping his fingers. Servants rushed from the inn. D'Artagnan fought bravely, but he was outnumbered. A second later, he was knocked unconscious with a frying pan.

D'Artagnan awoke with a bandage around his head. "How dare you attack a lord, in my inn?" the innkeeper shouted, jabbing a finger at him. "Get out!"

D'Artagnan leapt to his feet, then stopped. Outside the window, a beautiful young woman with blonde hair leant from the window of a carriage. The dark-haired lord who'd laughed at d'Artagnan was speaking to her. "You must go to England, immediately," he said. "I'll return to Paris."

D'Artagnan heard no more. Striding from the inn, he shouted, "This time you'll not escape!"

The lord turned, already drawing his sword. But the woman stopped him, saying, "There's no time for duels."

"You're right, Milady," the lord said, as her carriage rattled away. Ignoring d'Artagnan, he leapt on to his horse and galloped off, leaving d'Artagnan in a cloud of dust.

D'Artagnan stared after him. "You'll pay for your laughter, my lord," he whispered. "I'll find out who you are, and the lady, too."

∾ 2 Time to learn some manners ∾

A week later, d'Artagnan arrived in Paris. He made his way to the grand office of Captain Treville, where he bowed nervously in front of the captain of the King's Musketeers.

The captain was angry. The night before, three Musketeers – Porthos, Athos and Aramis – had fought with the guards of Minister Richelieu, the most powerful man in France after the King. Aramis had been wounded in the shoulder. The King was furious. D'Artagnan had to stand in the corner of the office while Captain Treville shouted at the three men.

After they left, Captain Treville listened while d'Artagnan asked to join the Musketeers. He shook his head. "I'm sorry, you're too young and inexperienced," he said. Seeing d'Artagnan's disappointment, he added, "But I can offer training. It would be a start."

"Thank you, sir." D'Artagnan bowed again. "I'll soon prove myself worthy."

Captain Treville nodded, liking the confident young man. "I'll write a letter," he said. "Take it to the Royal Academy to begin your training."

While the captain wrote, d'Artagnan stared out of the window. He gasped. Across the street was the dark-haired lord from the village inn! The letter forgotten, he yelled, "I'll have his blood this time!"

In three bounds he was out the door and immediately crashed into Athos, one of the Musketeers who'd just left Captain Treville's office. "Sorry!" he cried, pushing past.

A strong hand fell on d'Artagnan's shoulder. "You think that's a good enough apology?" asked Athos in a quiet voice.

"I said sorry," d'Artagnan replied.

"I'll teach you some manners," said Athos.

These words, from a Musketeer, could only mean one thing: a duel. "Very well," d'Artagnan answered over his shoulder as he raced away. "I'll meet you at midday."

Running fast,
d'Artagnan collided
with another
Musketeer at
the bottom of the
stairs. This man was
handsome, dressed
in lace and velvet
and gold, and had
a perfectly trimmed
moustache. D'Artagnan

recognised Porthos as he struggled to
untangle himself from the Musketeer's long cloak.

"Excuse me, I'm in a hurry!"

"You risk punishment for your rudeness,"
growled Porthos.

D'Artagnan was being challenged to another duel!
"I shall meet you at 1 o'clock, sir," he said, freeing
himself from the cloak and rushing into the street.

He was too late. His enemy had vanished.

As he stood in the dusty street, a tall, slim and pale
man d'Artagnan recognised from Captain Treville's
office as Aramis, dropped a handkerchief from his
pocket and quickly stepped on it.

D'Artagnan pulled it from beneath his boot. "You dropped this, sir," he said, politely.

Aramis jumped. "I didn't," he hissed.

Another Musketeer chuckled. "A lady's handkerchief? From an admirer, Aramis?"

"It's not mine," Aramis insisted, but the other Musketeers were walking away, laughing. "You've embarrassed me," Aramis scowled at d'Artagnan.

D'Artagnan scowled back. "I was trying to be helpful," he said. "And you lied. I saw the handkerchief fall from your pocket."

"There's only one way to settle this," replied Aramis. He tapped the hilt of his sword.

"Agreed," d'Artagnan replied. "At 2 o'clock."

D'Artagnan sighed as Aramis walked away. He'd lost his enemy and agreed to fight three Musketeers – France's most famous swordsmen.

ᘒ 3 Against the odds ᘒ

As the bells of Paris chimed midday, d'Artagnan arrived at the quiet, grassy spot where duels were fought. All three Musketeers were waiting. Athos, Porthos and Aramis looked at each other in surprise when they learnt they'd all arranged to fight the same boy. "The lad has courage," said Athos. Aramis and Porthos nodded.

"I must apologise," said d'Artagnan, bowing. "It's unlikely I'll survive to fight all three of you. One or two will be disappointed."

The Musketeers glanced at each other again: this time in admiration.

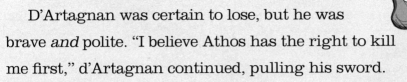

D'Artagnan was certain to lose, but he was brave *and* polite. "I believe Athos has the right to kill me first," d'Artagnan continued, pulling his sword.

As Athos drew his sword, d'Artagnan saw him wince. Remembering the Musketeer had been wounded in his right shoulder, he said, "If you like, sir, I'll wait until you've healed."

"Thank you, but I fight just as well with my left hand," replied Athos.

Swords crossed with a clash of steel, but at the same moment a troop of five men marched round the corner. "Richelieu's men!" Athos hissed. "Drop your sword."

D'Artagnan let his blade fall, but it was too late. The commander of Richelieu's guard had seen them. "Duelling's forbidden," he said, nastily. "You're all under arrest."

"Five of them, against three of us," whispered Athos to Porthos and Aramis. "We're outnumbered, but I refuse to be arrested by Richelieu's dogs."

Swords appeared in the hands of Porthos and Aramis.

D'Artagnan stepped over to stand beside the three Musketeers. "If I may correct you, Master Athos, there are *four* of us," he said.

"You're not a Musketeer," said Porthos.

D'Artagnan turned to face Richelieu's men. "But I have a Musketeer's heart," he replied.

"I knew you were a brave lad," said Athos with a wink. "What's your name?"

D'Artagnan just had time to shout his name before Richelieu's men advanced.

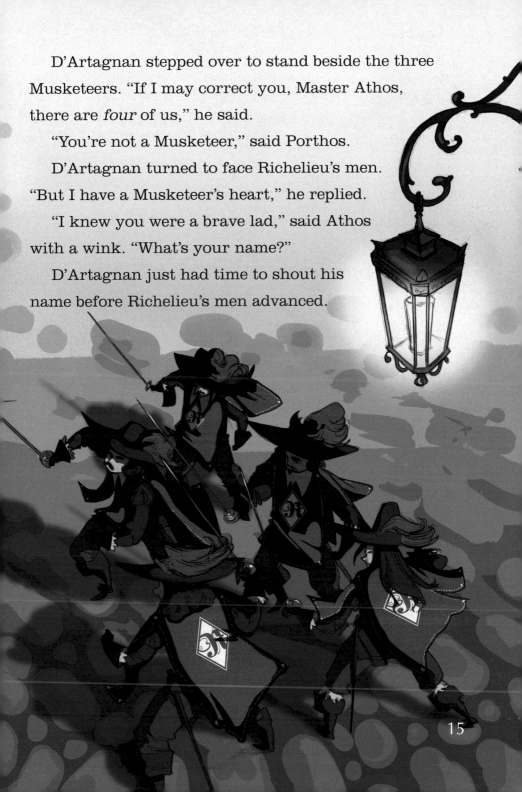

A moment later, d'Artagnan was fighting like a tiger. His opponent was older and stronger, but needed all his skill to defend himself. D'Artagnan whipped his sword around with blinding speed, dodging the other man's cuts.

"But you're just a boy," the man sneered, lunging.

D'Artagnan leapt aside, his blade flashing in the sunlight. Again and again, the commander struck. Each time, d'Artagnan dodged and struck back like lightning. The sound of steel against steel rang out. In fury, Richelieu's man lunged – his sword aimed at d'Artagnan's heart. D'Artagnan ducked beneath his blade and jabbed.

The man fell to the ground.

As d'Artagnan sprang to help Athos, he glanced at the other two Musketeers. Aramis stood victorious over his opponent. Porthos laughed, making jokes as his blade blurred through the air. "Excuse me. This one is mine," Athos said, stepping in front of d'Artagnan. A moment later, the guard lay dead.

Porthos's opponent was the last man standing. With a snarl, he turned and ran.

Shouting in triumph, the three Musketeers watched him flee and slapped d'Artagnan on the back, yelling congratulations. D'Artagnan's face split in a wide grin. He was on his way to becoming a Musketeer!

∾ 4 Trouble with diamonds ∾

After Porthos, Athos and Aramis told Captain Treville
how well d'Artagnan had fought, the Captain found him
a place in the King's Guards. Even better, he promised
him a place in the Musketeers after two years
of training.

D'Artagnan settled into his new life in Paris.
He hired a servant, called Planchet, and rented rooms in
the house of a businessman called Monsieur Bonacieux.
Every spare moment was spent with his new friends –
Athos, Porthos and Aramis.

A few weeks after the fight with Richelieu's men,
Bonacieux knocked at his door. "I'll pay the rent soon,"
d'Artagnan told him, though, in fact, he had spent all
his money.

"I'm not here for rent," the old man told him. "I heard you're a brave young man who's training to become a Musketeer and I need help."

"Help?" d'Artagnan asked, confused.

"My wife has been kidnapped," Bonacieux whispered. "She's the Queen's dressmaker. Richelieu has kidnapped my poor Constance so that he can question her about the Queen's secrets."

D'Artagnan's face went pale. It was well known that although the King and Minister Richelieu pretended to be friends, they were in fact bitter enemies. "How do you know?" he asked.

Bonacieux looked around, afraid of being overheard. "A man has been following her and I think he's taken her," he whispered. "A dark-haired man, with a scar on his cheek."

D'Artagnan jumped to his feet. This could only be the same man who'd laughed at him! "I'll find her," he declared. "The man who took her will die."

That evening d'Artagnan told his three friends Bonacieux's story.

"If Richelieu's taken an innocent woman, then we're at war with him," said Athos, sternly.

Stretching out a hand, he said: "All for one, and one for all!" In turn, Porthos, Aramis and d'Artagnan placed their hands on top of his. "All for one, and one for all!" they repeated.

For days, d'Artagnan and the Musketeers searched Paris, but Constance Bonacieux had disappeared. Meanwhile, Richelieu's spies had arrested Monsieur Bonacieux to stop him trying to find his wife and now watched his house. D'Artagnan began to lose hope of finding Constance until, one night, he heard a woman's voice crying for help in the room below his.

Instantly, he ran for the stairs and raced to his landlord's apartment. With a fierce cry, he kicked open the door, his sword a blur of sliver. Soon four men ran from the house, blood streaming from cuts made by d'Artagnan's blade.

D'Artagnan was alone with a pretty young woman who had dark hair and blue eyes. "You saved me," said Constance Bonacieux, taking his hands.

"Your husband said you'd been kidnapped," said D'Artagnan.

"I was imprisoned in a house, but I tied bedsheets together and climbed out of the window," Constance explained. "When I found my way home those men were here in my apartment."

"They're Richelieu's spies. They've been watching the house," d'Artagnan explained.

"I must find my husband," Constance said. "He has to go to England, immediately."

"Your husband's in prison," d'Artagnan told her. "Let me help instead."

"But I hardly know you," replied Constance.

D'Artagnan interrupted. "I serve the King and Queen," he said. "Trust me."

Constance looked at him. "It'll be dangerous," she said.

D'Artagnan smiled. "My friends will come with me," he said. "They're the best men of the King's Musketeers. No danger frightens them."

"Very well," said Constance. "I was kidnapped because I was trying to help the Queen with a terrible problem. The King gave her some diamond studs, but, secretly, the Queen presented the jewels as a gift to her friend, the English Duke of Buckingham. The King hates England. If he finds out …"

"The Queen will be in trouble and there might be war with England," d'Artagnan said.

"Yes," Constance nodded. "Richelieu discovered that the Duke has the diamonds. To stir up trouble he asked the King why the Queen never wears them, knowing she can't. Now, the King has ordered a ball to be held in twelve days, and told the Queen he expects to see the diamonds. If she doesn't wear them, it will be a catastrophe."

"Twelve days," d'Artagnan said, deep in thought. "Just enough time to get to London, fetch the diamonds and return."

"Richelieu knows everything. He'll try to stop you if he thinks you're going to get the diamonds from the Duke of Buckingham," said Constance.

But it was too late.

The door slammed. D'Artagnan was already on his way.

At 2 o'clock in the morning, four horses galloped
out of Paris. The four friends raced along moonlit
roads, cloaks streaming out behind them. As the sun
rose, they stopped at an inn for breakfast. As they
ate, a stranger joined their table. "A toast to Minister
Richelieu," said the man, raising his glass.

"I won't raise a glass to *him*," said Porthos.

"Raise a glass or you're dead," hissed the stranger,
jumping up with a sword in his hand.

"Leave," Porthos shouted to his friends. "This wretch
is one of Richelieu's spies, but d'Artagnan's mission
can't be interrupted."

The clash of steel on steel filled d'Artagnan's ears as he, Athos and Aramis galloped away, leaving Porthos to fight alone.

At midday, the three riders saw a gang of men mending the road ahead. As they slowed their horses, the workmen dropped their tools and scurried into the bushes. "Something's wrong!" yelled d'Artagnan.

A second later, shots rang out. "An ambush!" cried Aramis, as a bullet hit him in the shoulder. "Fly, Musketeers!"

Hooves pounding the road, three horses galloped through a hail of bullets. In the storm of gunpowder smoke and the crack of gun shots, d'Artagnan felt a bullet zip past his ear. Leaning over his horse's neck, he urged it on.

By the time they reached the safety of a small town. Aramis was slumped in his saddle. "I can't travel any further," he groaned, clutching his wounded shoulder. "Go on without me."

That night, d'Artagnan and Athos slept at another inn. But their troubles weren't over. At dawn, d'Artagnan was leaving their room when he heard raised voices. "These coins are fakes!" shouted the innkeeper. "Guards – arrest this man!"

"You dog!" shouted Athos. "Those coins aren't fakes!"

D'Artagnan heard shots being fired and raced to help his friend, sword in hand.

"Go!" yelled Athos. "It's another ambush. Ride, ride!"

Hours later, d'Artagnan arrived in the town of Calais. Of the four riders, only he had escaped unhurt and he still had to find a boat to take him to England.

"The port is closed by Richelieu's order. You must have permission to sail," the harbour master told him, pointing. "Follow that gentleman. He's taking his letter from Richelieu to the governor's house for approval."

Leaping back on to his exhausted horse, d'Artagnan spurred it on, and caught up with a thin, snooty-looking man. "Excuse me," said d'Artagnan, politely. "I must ask for your letter of permission to sail."

"Impossible," the man sneered. "I'm on business for Minister Richelieu."

"But I must have the letter," replied d'Artagnan, leaping from his horse.

"Then try to take it!" replied the man, drawing his sword.

The fight didn't last long. D'Artagnan fought with furious skill and as the man fell to the ground, d'Artagnan pulled the precious letter from his coat.

The following day, d'Artagnan's ship sailed up
the River Thames into the bustling docks of London.
Alone in a strange city, he quickly found his way to
Buckingham Palace – home of the Duke of Buckingham.
He bowed to a tall, good-looking man with long, curled
hair and a gold-embroidered coat. "I come on an urgent
mission from the Queen of France," he told the Duke.

"Is something wrong?" Buckingham asked, his face
suddenly pale.

"The Queen is in grave danger." D'Artagnan told Buckingham about Richelieu's plot. "So, I must take the diamonds back," he finished.

"There's no time to waste," the Duke agreed. "Follow me."

A few moments later d'Artagnan stared down into a jewel case where diamonds glittered. The Duke couldn't believe his eyes. "It's not possible. There were twelve. Now there are only ten."

"Who could have stolen two?" asked d'Artagnan.

The Duke growled, "Milady, the Countess de Winter. I wore the diamonds to a ball last week and danced with her. She must have cut two from my coat."

With a groan, d'Artagnan remembered the woman his dark-haired, scarred enemy had called "Milady" weeks earlier. Now he understood why she'd been told to go to England. "The Countess de Winter," he said. "Is she a beautiful woman with blonde hair?"

The Duke nodded.

"Milady must be one of Richelieu's spies," d'Artagnan told him. "She must have taken the diamonds to him. Now, when the Queen fails to wear all twelve, Richelieu will be able to show them to the King and tell him where they came from."

"Unless we can replace them," said the Duke, brightening. Turning to a servant, he said, "Fetch the best jeweller in London, immediately."

An hour later, a bald old man peered through a magnifying glass at the ten diamonds. "These are exquisite," he murmured, "but yes, my lord, I can cut two exactly the same."

"Finish the job within five days and I'll pay you double whatever you ask," said the Duke. He turned to d'Artagnan. "You'll have three days to return to Paris. Will it be enough?"

With a gulp, d'Artagnan nodded.

❦ 6 A meeting with the Minister ↶

"So, the Queen danced with the King wearing all twelve diamonds," said Captain Treville. "Richelieu was so furious he stormed out of the ball. The Queen's sent Constance Bonacieux into hiding in case he decides to punish her."

The three Musketeers and d'Artagnan smiled. They'd beaten Richelieu! Porthos, Athos and Aramis had escaped their attackers with only small wounds and soon returned to Paris. D'Artagnan looked down at the diamond ring that the Queen of France had given him to thank him for his service.

"But, back to business," the Captain continued. "The town of La Rochelle has been taken by traitors to the King. Porthos, Aramis and Athos will ride there with the Musketeers. D'Artagnan, you'll ride with the King's Guards."

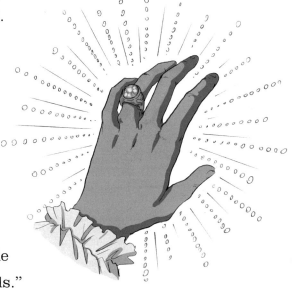

Over the following days, d'Artagnan and the Musketeers prepared for battle. On the last day before they left Paris for La Rochelle, d'Artagnan heard a knock at the door. Opening it, he found himself face to face with one of Minister Richelieu's guards. Without a word, the man handed him a note. Richelieu himself wanted to see him!

Hardly daring to think what dungeon might await him, he ran to tell his friends.

"Don't worry," said Athos, clapping d'Artagnan on the shoulder, "the three of us will wait outside. If you don't come out we'll storm the palace."

D'Artagnan bowed as he was shown into Minister Richelieu's office. Looking up, he saw a slim man in plain clothes with a pointed beard.

Minister Richelieu leant on his desk and gave him a cool look. "You're d'Artagnan?" he asked.

"Yes, my lord," d'Artagnan replied.

"The same d'Artagnan who fought with a dark-haired, scarred man last month? The same d'Artagnan who was told by Constance Bonacieux of some missing diamonds?"

D'Artagnan's eyes widened as the Minister went on listing details of his life. How could he know so much? "You're correct," he said, finally.

He felt sure he was going to be arrested, but then Richelieu astounded him. "You showed courage and intelligence, both of which I admire. I offer you a place in my guard."

D'Artagnan's jaw dropped open. "But I ... I ... want to be a Musketeer," he stuttered.

"You refuse?" Richelieu looked stern.

"My friends are Musketeers," said d'Artagnan quickly. "If I joined your guard I'd become their enemy and I've already fought your men. They'll not welcome me."

"So be it," growled Richelieu with a scowl, "but I give you this warning: your refusal offends me and I'm a dangerous enemy."

⟪ 7 For King and Queen ⟫

"Hoy! D'Artagnan!"

After his meeting with Richelieu, d'Artagnan and his servant Planchet had ridden to La Rochelle with the King's Guards, but his Musketeer friends had beaten him there. D'Artagnan turned to see a familiar, grinning face. "Porthos!" he yelled, happily.

"Come quickly!" shouted Porthos.

D'Artagnan cheerfully joined Porthos, Aramis and Athos.

"We have news," said Athos. "On our way here we stopped at an inn – "

"Where we overheard a man and a woman talking," Porthos interrupted.

"It was Richelieu and a woman. He's sent her to assassinate the Duke of Buckingham."

D'Artagnan's eyes opened wide in shock. "It must have been Milady!" he exclaimed.

Athos nodded. "She's taken a ship to England."

"We must warn the Duke," d'Artagnan said.

"Why?" asked Porthos. "England's our enemy."

"He's the Queen's friend," d'Artagnan replied.

"But we can't leave La Rochelle – we're here to fight," said Aramis.

Athos looked thoughtful. "A letter," he said. "With luck, a fast rider might arrive in England before Milady."

"Planchet!" d'Artagnan said. "He can take a letter to the Duke and warn him."

Hurriedly they wrote a letter and ordered Planchet to ride like the wind and deliver it.

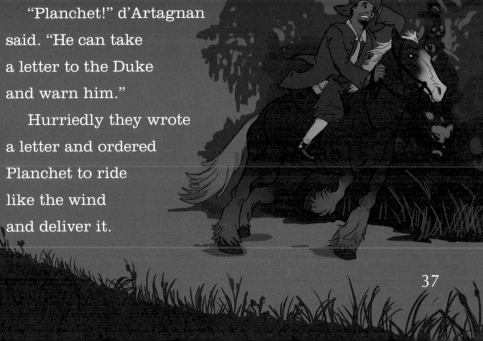

While Planchet was gone, d'Artagnan and
the Musketeers fought bravely against the traitors at
La Rochelle. As bullets zipped around their ears, they
climbed through the remains of a fort outside the town
and bravely killed 22 traitors.

The tale of their heroic efforts spread quickly.
Soon, even the King, who'd travelled to La Rochelle,
heard about them and commanded Captain Treville
to make d'Artagnan a Musketeer.

At last! d'Artagnan had proved himself and joined
the finest soldiers in France. In his new uniform,
he should've been overjoyed, but d'Artagnan
couldn't stop thinking about Planchet and the fate of
the Duke of Buckingham.

After two weeks, d'Artagnan was certain that
Planchet had been caught by Richelieu's spies.
With a sigh, he stood alone in the dark outside an inn.
Soldiers' laughter drifted from the open windows.
He'd failed.

"It's cold, sir," said a voice
behind him. "I brought your cloak."

"Planchet!" D'Artganan spun round and hugged his
servant. "Thank goodness you're safe. Tell me – quickly
– what happened?"

"I've a letter for you, sir."

D'Artagnan opened it with trembling fingers and
read the Duke's reply: "Thank you; be easy," was all it
said. He grinned. The Duke was safe!

"Milady's in prison," Planchet told him, bowing.

8 The swift hand of justice

After two weeks, the traitors of La Rochelle
surrendered. Outnumbered by the King's army
and outwitted by the cunning Richelieu, their only other
choices were to starve within the walls of their city,
or to face certain death on the battlefield. Triumphant,
the King returned to Paris. His Musketeers rode at
his side as a guard.

At home, d'Artagnan found a message waiting for
him. The Queen wished him to take a letter to Constance
Bonacieux, who was still in hiding. "We'll come too,"
Athos insisted. "The roads are dangerous."

"You worry too much," d'Artagnan laughed.

A day later, he wasn't laughing. The four Musketeers
arrived at the house where Constance was hidden,
just in time to see a carriage rattle away at high speed.
Something was wrong!

D'Artagnan felt a freezing hand grip his heart. "Constance! Where is she?" he yelled, as he burst through the front door.

An old lady blinked at him. "Upstairs," she said, "talking with another lady ..."

D'Artagnan leapt up the stairs three at a time. Shouldering his way through the door, he cried out in horror. Constance lay on the floor. D'Artagnan threw himself to his knees, speaking gently. "It's all right," he said, "I'll fetch a doctor."

"D'Artagnan, is that you?" Constance whispered, looking up. "A woman came. She said she was your friend."

"Her name? What was her name?" d'Artagnan's voice croaked.

"She poured me a drink," whispered Constance. "It must've been poisoned."

"But what was her name?"

"Her name?" whispered Constance. "She called herself the Countess de Winter."

With these words, she closed her eyes and stopped breathing.

Horses sweating, the Musketeers followed the darkening road that Milady's carriage had taken until they reached a small village. After questioning the villagers, Athos said, "We rest here."

"But we'll lose Milady," d'Artagnan protested.

"No," Athos replied. "It'll soon be dark and the villagers say she's stopped a little further down the road. Our servants can watch while I find someone we'll need when we catch up with her."

At dawn, the Musketeers continued. Riding alongside them was a stranger in a hooded red cloak. D'Artagnan tried to speak to him, but the man stayed silent. At the next village, Athos pointed to a cottage by a river. Milady's carriage stood outside.

Minutes later, d'Artagnan kicked in the door, Aramis and Porthos close behind him. Athos leapt in through the window. Surprised, Milady drew a dagger and hurled herself at d'Artagnan. Instantly, she was staring down the blades of four swords.

"Drop the dagger," said Porthos.

Milady's dagger clattered to the floor.

"How did you escape?" d'Artagnan growled. "We thought you were a prisoner."

Milady tossed her head and looked at d'Artagnan scornfully. "It was easy for a woman as beautiful as me," she said with a smile.

"I persuaded the guard to let me go and then I sent him to kill the Duke of Buckingham."

The Musketeers gasped. "The Duke is dead?" said Porthos.

"Yes," said Milady, "and now I've killed Constance Bonacieux, too, for daring to interfere with Richelieu's plans! Richelieu will soon execute you as well, d'Artagnan."

"You'll never see Richelieu again," said Athos "I charge you with the murder of Constance Bonacieux."

A scowl crossed Milady's face. "You're not a judge. You can't put me on trial."

At last, the man in red walked through the
door and pushed back his hood. He had a face like
stone. "These Musketeers may not have the power
to judge you, lady, but I do," he said. "I'm the judge
and executioner of this district and I heard you confess
to murder. You'll be punished immediately."

Seeing she'd made a terrible mistake in admitting her
guilt, Milady trembled. Her knees buckled beneath her.
"Help me," she pleaded to d'Artagnan, as she dropped
to the floor. "Don't let him take me. Richelieu will
reward you."

D'Artagnan turned away.

∾ 9 All for one, and one for all! ↝

Grim-faced, the Musketeers rode back to Paris.
As they approached the city, a man rode towards them.
D'Artagnan saw that it was the dark-haired lord with
the scar. He drew his sword.

"You'll not need that," the man sneered. "I'm under
orders from Minister Richelieu to arrest you."

D'Artagnan put away his sword. "Then take me to
him," he said.

Richelieu frowned as d'Artagnan was led, once again, into his office. "I warned you not to make an enemy of me," he said, "yet you've meddled with my plans again."

"Who says I meddled?" replied d'Artagnan, calm and cool. "Milady, the Countess de Winter? She's a murderer, my lord."

Richelieu blinked. "If that's true, she'll face trial," he muttered.

"My friends and I brought her before a judge already," d'Artagnan replied. "She's paid for her crime with her life."

"She's dead?" Richelieu looked shocked.

D'Artagnan nodded. Quickly, he told Richelieu all that had happened. "Punish me if you wish, but I'm not sorry."

Without another word, Richelieu sat and began writing. After a few moments, he handed the paper to d'Artagnan.

Certain that it was an order for his own execution, d'Artagnan trembled as he began to read. Then his jaw fell open. The paper was a promotion, with a blank space. Next to the King, Richelieu was the most powerful man in France. So powerful, in fact, that he could give any orders he wished – even to the Musketeers. Captain Treville would have to obey. Whoever added their name to the paper that d'Artagnan now held would become a lieutenant in the Musketeers.

"You're not imprisoning me?" d'Artagnan said, confused.

"I can't punish you on the word of a convicted murderer," said Richelieu. "But again you've proved yourself brave and intelligent, even if you did try to ruin my plans. Such courage should be rewarded."

"But … but what about Milady?" d'Artagnan stammered.

Minister Richelieu looked thoughtful. "I'm sometimes harsh because I protect France," he said, "but I wouldn't order the murder of an innocent woman. The Countess de Winter was acting alone and justice has been done."

D'Artagnan opened his mouth to speak. "There's one more thing," Richelieu interrupted. In a louder voice, he called a name.

The dark-haired lord with a scar entered the room. D'Artagnan glared at him.

Richelieu looked from one to the other. "This is the Chevalier de Rochefort, d'Artagnan. I promise you he had nothing to do with the death of Constance Bonacieux. The two of you will put aside your fight, by *my* order."

D'Artagnan couldn't help scowling, but he bowed to de Rochefort. "I'll not forget our quarrel," he murmured.

"Nor I," whispered Rochefort.

"Now go," said Richelieu. "Both of you."

D'Artagnan found Porthos, Aramis and Athos and waved the piece of paper Richelieu had given him. "There's no name," he told the three Musketeers, breathlessly. "One of you must sign it."

"Not I," said Athos. "You earnt this promotion, d'Artagnan."

"Nor I," said Porthos, smoothing his moustache. "If I was a lieutenant I wouldn't have time to see to my clothes."

"I'll not take it either," added Aramis. "You'll make a better lieutenant than any of us, d'Artagnan."

Athos took Richelieu's letter and added d'Artagnan's name. "There, it's done," he said. "All that's left is to order the best dinner France has ever seen in honour of our new commander, Monsieur d'Artagnan."

"All for one," said Aramis, stretching out his sword.

One by one, the other Musketeers placed their swords on top of his. "And one for all!" they shouted together.

Musketeer skills

Loyalty

"I serve the King and the Queen."

Courage

At 2 o'clock in the morning, four horses galloped out of Paris.

Intelligence

"Milady must be one of Richelieu's spies."

Bravery

They climbed through
the remains of a fort.

Swordsmanship

D'Artagnan whipped his
sword around with
blinding speed.

Friendship

"All for one,
and one for all!"

Ideas for reading

Written by Clare Dowdall, PhD
Lecturer and Primary Literacy Consultant

Reading objectives:
- ask questions to improve their understanding
- summarise the main ideas drawn from more than one paragraph, identifying key details that support the main ideas
- explain and discuss their understanding of what they have read

Spoken language objectives:
- participate in discussions, presentations, performances, role play, improvisations and debates

Curriculum Links: Geography – locational knowledge

Resources: dictionary, art materials for making a banner, pencils and paper/ ICT for making an advert

Build a context for reading
- Show the front cover and ask children to suggest what a Musketeer is. Look up the word "musket/musketeer" in a dictionary to check its meaning.
- Read the blurb to the group. Ask children to make deductions and predictions about the story based upon the information provided.
- Explain that this is a retelling of a classic story by Alexandre Dumas. Ask if any children know about the original story and help them to think about the setting and historical context from the information given.

Understand and apply reading strategies
- Explain that reading involves making rich pictures in your mind and asking questions about the story. Ask children to do this as they read Chapter 1.
- Ask children to recount some key moments from the opening chapter and to raise questions about the developing story, e.g. *Who's the dark haired stranger?*